The Mystery of the African Gray

THREE COUSINS DETECTIVE CLUB®

The Mystery of the African Gray

Elspeth Campbell Murphy

Illustrated by Joe Nordstrom

BETHANY HOUSE PUBLISHERS
MINNEAPOLIS, MINNESOTA 55438

Published by Bethany House Publishers
A Ministry of Bethany Fellowship International
11300 Hampshire Avenue South
Minneapolis, Minnesota 55438
www.bethanyhouse.com

Printed in the United States of America by
Bethany Press International, Minneapolis, Minnesota 55438

Library of Congress Cataloging-in-Publication Data

CIP data applied for

ISBN 0–7642–2130–2   CIP

ELSPETH CAMPBELL MURPHY has been a familiar name in Christian publishing for over fifteen years, with more than seventy-five books to her credit and sales reaching five million worldwide. She is the author of the best-selling series *David and I Talk to God* and *The Kids From Apple Street Church*, as well as the 1990 Gold Medallion winner *Do You See Me, God?*, and two books of prayer meditations for teachers, *Chalkdust* and *Recess*. A graduate of Trinity College and Moody Bible Institute, Elspeth and her husband, Mike, make their home in Chicago, where she writes full time.

Contents

"People enjoy giving good answers! Saying the right word at the right time is so pleasing!"
Proverbs 15:23

1

George Washington Is Missing

When Titus McKay answered the phone that Saturday morning, his two visiting cousins, Timothy Dawson and Sarah-Jane Cooper, couldn't help listening in.

Titus said to the person on the phone, "OK, I'll check with my mom and then we'll be right down to help you find him. . . . Yeah, Timothy and Sarah-Jane are here, too. . . . OK. Bye."

Titus called to his mother, "Mom, Mrs. Simpson says George Washington is missing and she wants us to help her look for him."

"All right," said his mother. "But be careful. I don't trust that guy."

9

"Oh, he's OK," Titus replied. "He just acts like a spoiled brat sometimes. But don't worry. We'll be careful." To his cousins he said, "You guys *do* want to come, right?"

Throughout this whole conversation, Timothy and Sarah-Jane had been staring at Titus openmouthed.

It was if they were all having the same really weird dream. There you were, looking for something. And it turned out that the "thing" you were looking for was George Washington. The First President. The Father of His Country. Only—he was acting like a spoiled brat. And your aunt was there, too. And she was saying, "I don't trust that guy!"

Totally weird.

Except Titus was acting as if nothing weird was happening at all.

What was going on here?

Titus saw the looks on their faces and burst out laughing. "I'll explain on the way," he said.

2

The T.C.D.C.

*T*itus hurried his cousins down the hall to the elevators and pushed the Down button.

But when the elevator came, Sarah-Jane refused to get on. She said, "Titus Gordon McKay! I am not going one step farther until you tell us what this is all about!"

"And it had better be a logical explanation!" added Timothy.

"George Washington is a *parrot*," said Titus. "A beautiful African gray. Smart as a whip. Now all we have to do is find him."

"Why? What happened?" asked Timothy.

"Mrs. Simpson let him out of his cage for some exercise," said Titus. "And now he's missing."

They rode down three floors to the sixteenth floor.

Titus knocked on the door of Mrs. Simpson's apartment and announced, "The T.C.D.C. at your service."

This was not the first time the three cousins had helped Mrs. Simpson look for something.

Mrs. Simpson was a very intelligent lady. Even though she was almost as old as the cousins' grandparents, she had decided to go to college. She was a student at the university where Titus's father taught. But—smart as she was—Mrs. Simpson was also kind of absent-minded. She was always misplacing things. So she had asked for the cousins' help before. Although—this was the first time she had misplaced a parrot.

The first time Mrs. Simpson heard about the T.C.D.C., she had asked, "What's a 'teesy-deesy'?"

And Titus had explained, "It's letters. Capital T. Capital C. Capital D. Capital C. It stands for the Three Cousins Detective Club."

So of course now Mrs. Simpson knew that when it came to finding things, no one was better at it than Timothy, Titus, and Sarah-Jane.

3

A Flying Toddler

"I'm so glad you were home, Titus!" exclaimed Mrs. Simpson as she opened the door. "And Timothy! Sarah-Jane! It's so nice to see you again. I really appreciate your help."

"We didn't know *what* was going on at first!" said Timothy. "But then Titus gave us the logical explanation."

"A *parrot*," said Sarah-Jane. "Named *George Washington*." She sounded as if she thought she was still dreaming.

"I know," said Mrs. Simpson as she led them into the apartment and they began to look around. "That wouldn't have been my choice for a name, either. But my uncle always claimed the bird looked just like George

Washington. I never could see it, though. Could you, Titus?"

Titus shook his head. Then he added, "Well, maybe a *little* bit. If you really, *really* use your imagination."

"Well, that's something my uncle had plenty of!" declared Mrs. Simpson.

"Your uncle?" asked Sarah-Jane. "You mean, the parrot isn't yours?"

Mrs. Simpson sighed and gave a sad little smile. "He is now. You see, George belonged to my dear uncle Henry, who suddenly passed away not too long ago. So I am now the—um—proud owner of an African gray."

Titus said to his cousins, "That often happens. Parrots outliving their owners, I mean. That's because parrots can live such a long time. Eighty years, maybe. So if the owner dies, someone else has to take care of the parrot.

"And that can be kind of hard on the parrot because they usually have just one favorite person—even if they like other people, too. But George is lucky. He already knows Mrs. Simpson from all the times she visited Uncle Henry. George will never forget Uncle Henry because parrots have *amazing* memories. But Mrs. Simpson will get to be George's favorite person now. He knows me, too, because I used to go along to visit sometimes."

"George is absolutely crazy about you, Titus," said Mrs. Simpson with a smile. To Timothy and Sarah-Jane she said, "Your cousin Titus has been a big help to me. When I'm super busy, I hire him to come pay attention to George Washington for me. George Washington can be such a brat when he thinks he's not getting enough attention."

It still sounded funny to Timothy and Sarah-Jane to hear someone talking about George Washington that way. But they knew what she meant.

And it was not at all surprising to them to hear that Titus was helping out with a fussy parrot. Titus had a special way with animals. He loved them and they loved him. Animals who wouldn't go to anyone else would go to Titus.

But so far, not even Titus had been able to find Mr. Washington.

Mrs. Simpson sighed. "I just turned my back for a minute, and he was gone."

"He sounds like a toddler," said Timothy, who had a busy little sister.

"That's it exactly!" agreed Mrs. Simpson. "A toddler. A toddler who can fly."

Timothy gulped. The idea of a flying toddler was too horrible to even think about.

Mrs. Simpson said, "I want George to get used to his new home. But it's hard to be patient when I'm so busy trying to organize my uncle's things. Uncle Henry could be so absentminded!" She stopped and thought about this. "Dear me!" she said. "That sounds just like me, doesn't it? I guess it runs in the family. But I just *know* there's something important Uncle Henry forgot to tell me."

Before they could think anymore about this, they were interrupted.

By someone singing, "I'm a Yankee Doodle Dandy."

The singing was coming from the kitchen.

But when they rushed in, there was no one there.

4

One Smart Parrot

*T*o everyone's amazement, the singing seemed to be coming from one of the kitchen cupboards. The one where the door stood slightly open.

Quietly—so as not to frighten the parrot—Titus stood on the kitchen step stool and peeked in.

There was George Washington, perched happily on the edge of a big pot. Apparently he had figured out how to open the door all by himself. He had also figured out how to crawl inside and pull the door almost shut behind him. He was one smart bird, all right.

Titus wasn't sure what to say.

He didn't want to call George a bad bird because George probably had no idea he

18

wasn't supposed to be there.

But neither did Titus want to tell George how smart he was for figuring all this out. Maybe Mrs. Simpson didn't want him in the kitchen cupboards.

So Titus just said matter-of-factly, "Hi, George."

"Hi, Titus!" came the friendly reply.

"I just love when he does that!" Titus whispered to his cousins and Mrs. Simpson.

Realizing that there were other people below, George Washington pushed the door open farther and peeked out.

He squawked in alarm at the sight of two strangers in his kitchen.

"Don't be scared, George," said Titus soothingly. "They're with me. These are my cousins, Timothy and Sarah-Jane." He turned to his cousins and whispered, "He likes people, but he's very shy."

George Washington cocked his head, looked down at Sarah-Jane, and said loudly, "Hi ya, toots!"

"He sure doesn't *sound* shy!" muttered Sarah-Jane.

George looked right at Timothy, thought about it for a minute, and said, "Hi, Titus."

Then Mr. Washington crept back farther into his cupboard, reached up, and pulled the door almost shut.

"*Now* what do we do?" asked Mrs. Simpson. "We can't force him to come down."

"No," said Titus. "That would only scare him." He reached up and nudged open the cupboard a little. "George," he said. "We're all going into the living room. Why don't you come join us when you're ready? We'd love to see some of the tricks you can do on your climbing tree. OK?"

George cocked his head and considered carefully what Titus was saying. " 'Twas the night before Christmas," he replied.

"Aurrggh!" said Titus softly. "What a bird!"

"What a bird," agreed George Washington.

5

The Mysterious Bird-Word

*T*hey all went into the living room and sat down, waiting for George Washington to appear.

It didn't take long. George was unable to resist being at the center of things. He came waddling into the room as if he owned the place. He had a clumsy roly-poly way of walking that was great for tree branches but looked funny on the ground. Titus thought it was really kind of sweet.

Titus already had a sweet animal at home—his little Yorkshire terrier, Gubbio. Gubbio and Titus always seemed to know what the other was thinking. But Gubbio didn't actually *talk*. There was something so exciting to Titus about an animal that said real *words* . . .

"Hi, George," Titus said.

"Hi, George," replied the parrot.

. . . whether he understood them or not.

Titus sighed. Sometimes it seemed that George was actually having a conversation with you. Other times it seemed that he was just—well, "parroting" words he had heard.

"*I'm* not George," Titus told him. "*You're* George!"

George paused. He seemed to be giving this some serious thought. Then he hopped up to his climbing tree and looked with birdly satisfaction at his people. He had something important to tell them.

"Merry Christmas, everybody!"

"No, George," said Mrs. Simpson. "You're a few months off. This is *September*. Not *December*."

George Washington bobbed his head up and down as if he was agreeing with every word.

Then he looked at Mrs. Simpson and said, "Hi ya, toots!"

Sarah-Jane laughed. "Are you *toots*, too?"

"I guess so," said Mrs. Simpson. "He's not very respectful, is he?"

As if to prove her point, George flew over to the end table beside Titus's chair and said in a very demanding voice, "Fenway!"

"There's that word again!" exclaimed Mrs. Simpson. "It's the one thing he says that I can't understand at all. He's been saying it since he got here. What does it mean, Titus?"

Titus looked at Mrs. Simpson in surprise. "I was just going to ask you the same thing."

6

Peanuts

Whatever the strange word meant, George seemed to be pretty agitated about it.

He hopped on Titus's shoulder and screeched in his ear, "Fenway! Fenway! Fenway!"

"All right, already!" cried Titus. "Break my eardrums, why don't you?"

"Fenway," muttered George as he climbed down to the arm of the chair and began poking in Titus's pocket.

"Quit it, George!" said Titus. "What are you doing?"

Suddenly it hit him.

He wasn't a member of the T.C.D.C. for nothing.

Peanuts.

Titus's apartment building was right next to a city park. So Titus always carried peanuts in his pocket for the squirrels.

"George wants the peanuts," he said to Mrs. Simpson. "Is it all right for him to have them?"

Mrs. Simpson grabbed the parrot handbook and looked it up.

"Yes!" she said with relief. "Peanuts in the shell are all right as a special treat."

Everyone was relieved. No one wanted to be the one to tell George he couldn't have peanuts if he wanted peanuts.

Titus emptied his pockets and put the peanuts on the end table.

"Is this all right?" he asked Mrs. Simpson. "I don't want him messing up your furniture."

"Actually, he's pretty good about not doing that," Mrs. Simpson replied. "Though he does seem to like that end table. Who knows why? It's right across from his cage, so maybe he likes to look at it. It's one of a set. The other one is in Uncle Henry's living room."

George nibbled happily on the peanuts, occasionally looking up at Titus to say "Fenway."

When the peanuts were all gone, Titus said

loudly and clearly, "ALL GONE, George. All gone." Then he added under his breath, "And I don't want any arguments about it."

"All gone?" asked George meekly.

Titus had heard him say this before, and he seemed to know what it meant.

"Yes, George," said Titus firmly. "*All gone.*"

"Too bad," said George.

He flew back to his cage and climbed in.

Mrs. Simpson closed the door, and George didn't object at all.

"Whew!" she said. "What a morning! You kids were such a big help!"

"No problem," said Timothy.

"Think nothing of it," said Sarah-Jane.

"I wish I knew what *fenway* meant," said Titus.

7

Fenway??

"**W**hat makes you think *fenway* means anything at all, Ti?" asked Timothy curiously. "Doesn't George just—you know, *say* stuff? He says 'Merry Christmas,' but he doesn't know what month it is."

"Merry Christmas, everybody!" said George Washington.

"See what I mean?" asked Timothy.

"Hi, Titus!" said George, looking right at Timothy.

"Hi, George!" said Timothy and Titus together. They weren't even going to *try* to straighten him out on that one.

"You're right that George just says stuff," began Titus.

But he was interrupted by the ringing of

the phone. Mrs. Simpson went to answer it. The odd thing was that the phone went right on ringing—even after she picked up the receiver.

That's because it wasn't the phone.

It was George.

"Oh!" cried Mrs. Simpson. "He does that to me all the time. It's enough to drive me crazy."

"Hello?" said George. "Hello? Hello? Who's calling?"

"No one's calling, you silly bird," said Mrs. Simpson. But the cousins could tell by her tone of voice that she was already very attached to him.

"Anyway, as I was saying before being so rudely interrupted," began Titus, looking straight at George. "George says a lot of stuff. Sometimes it sounds like he knows what he's talking about, and sometimes it doesn't. But the point is, he *imitates* what he hears. He doesn't make stuff up. If he can say *fenway*, it's because Uncle Henry *taught* him to say *fenway*. Or it could be that George just heard the word so many times he picked it up."

"But that's what puzzles me," said Mrs.

Simpson. "I've *never* heard Uncle Henry use the word *fenway*. I have absolutely no idea what it means."

"Neither do I," said Titus. "And there's something else funny."

"Funny ha-ha or funny weird?" asked Timothy.

"Funny weird," said Titus.

"What's funny weird?" asked Sarah-Jane.

"The way George went after those peanuts," said Titus.

"Yes, that struck me as odd, too," said Mrs. Simpson.

"Why?" asked Sarah-Jane.

"Hi ya, toots!" said George Washington.

"Because parrots are very cautious about trying something new," said Mrs. Simpson. "George wouldn't eat something he hadn't seen before. That means Uncle Henry must have given him peanuts for a treat. I didn't know that."

"It seems like there's a lot we don't know," said Titus.

"A mystery?" asked Timothy.

The cousins always perked up when they

thought something mysterious might be going on.

"Why is the parrot saying *fenway*?" said Sarah-Jane.

"It's a silly little mystery," said Titus.

He was wrong about that.

8

An Unexpected Visitor

Solving mysteries was not the only work Titus did. He had a reputation in his building for being an excellent "gofer." People who had errands to run would often hire Titus to "go for" them. And because he was so dependable, he got other jobs, too. Dog walking, which he loved. Baby-sitting, which was usually fine. Even helping with housework, which was sometimes boring but more fun than doing his own room.

Titus wasn't getting rich, exactly. But he was doing OK.

He wasn't surprised when Mrs. Simpson said she wanted to hire him to help her clear out Uncle Henry's apartment. To at least get started on it, anyway. She said a job like that was much better with company.

Titus understood what she meant. It wasn't that Uncle Henry never threw *anything* away. . . . But pretty close. Titus wasn't sure how much help he would be. But he knew that Mrs. Simpson didn't want to face that huge job alone.

In fact, Mrs. Simpson wanted to hire Timothy and Sarah-Jane, too.

So the cousins called Titus's mother, and she said it would be OK.

Uncle Henry's apartment was in another building. So the plan was to take a bus over there, get some take-out hamburgers for lunch, and just see what they could get done in a couple of hours.

But things don't always go according to plan.

They were just getting ready to leave when the telephone rang. Mrs. Simpson laughed and said, "Oh, no, you don't, Mr. Washington! I'm not falling for *that* old trick again!"

But then George started muttering to himself about what a good bird he was. And the phone kept ringing.

So of course they knew it wasn't George. This time.

Titus was closest to the phone. So Mrs. Simpson asked him to get it. Again, Timothy and Sarah-Jane couldn't help listening in.

"Mrs. Simpson's residence. . . . Oh, hi, John. This is Titus. We're just on our way out. . . . *What* did you say? . . . Uh, OK. Just a second. I'll get her."

Titus handed the phone to Mrs. Simpson, and his cousins swooped down on him to find out what was going on.

"That was John, the doorman," Titus whispered. "He said Mrs. Simpson has a visitor downstairs who wants to come up and talk to her."

"What's so unusual about that?" asked Timothy softly.

"Yeah, Ti," whispered Sarah-Jane. "You look as if something really weird is happening."

"It is," replied Titus. "The visitor's name is Fenway."

9

Questions

"*T*hank you, John," said Mrs. Simpson speaking into the phone. "You can send her right up."

She put down the receiver and turned to the cousins. "Well!" she exclaimed. "You never know what a day's going to hold, do you?"

Sarah-Jane gave a puzzled frown. "But you don't even *know* anyone named Fenway, do you, Mrs. Simpson? Because when George said 'Fenway,' you would have thought of that person right away. Right?"

"That's right. I would have," replied Mrs. Simpson. "And I don't remember Uncle Henry mentioning anyone by that name."

"And yet—he taught George to say

37

'Fenway,' " mused Timothy. "So he must have known somebody named that."

Mrs. Simpson could only shrug. "This young woman's name is Karen Fenway. I'm sure she'll be able to help us with all our questions."

Titus was so curious he wanted to run out into the hall and wait by the elevator for this mysterious visitor.

But he figured that would look a little silly.

From the way Sarah-Jane was twisting her hair and Timothy was swinging his arms, Titus could tell they were as impatient as he was.

It seemed like a hundred years before they heard a timid knock on the door.

Mrs. Simpson hurried to answer it as the cousins tried mightily to keep from hopping up and down.

Karen Fenway turned out to be a nice-looking young woman with a sweet smile and a soft voice. She seemed a little shy.

That's probably why she jumped about a foot in the air when a loud voice screeched at her, "Hi ya, toots!"

Karen gasped and clapped her hand over her heart. "Goodness! What was *that*?"

"Oh, that's just George Washington," said Titus, reminding her of something she must already know. Any friend of Uncle Henry's would certainly know about George.

Karen stared at him. "*Who?*"

"George Washington," repeated Sarah-Jane, sounding almost as puzzled as Karen. "He lives here now, you know."

"He talks about you all the time," added Timothy.

Karen Fenway gave her head a little shake as if she were trying to wake up from a crazy dream.

"I'm sorry," she began. "But I'm just not following any of this. . . ."

"HI YA, TOOTS!"

"Oh!" cried Karen, laughing as she spotted George for the first time. "It's a *parrot!*"

"Of course it's a parrot," said Titus, feeling a little foggy himself. "It's *George Washington!*"

"Cute name!" said Karen. "How did you come up with it?"

"My uncle named him," said Mrs. Simpson. "Do you mean that you've never met George?"

"No," said Karen, looking more confused

than ever. "Why—um, why would you think I'd met your parrot?"

"Because he keeps saying 'Fenway,' " explained Timothy.

"I think we'd better all sit down before Karen *falls* down!" said Mrs. Simpson, seeing the look on Karen's face.

"Good idea!" said Karen. "Then I'm sure you'll be able to help me with all my questions."

10

More Questions

Naturally, the more they tried to get George to say "Fenway," the more he refused to say it.

"Oh, well," sighed Mrs. Simpson after they had all introduced themselves. "You're just going to have to take our word for it that this silly bird says 'Fenway.' "

"Oh, I believe you!" Karen replied. "But why would my name be one of George's words? I don't understand it. You see, I never met your uncle Henry. I was just told to go and see him because he was keeping something for me. But when I got there, a neighbor told me that he had passed away and that maybe you could help me, Mrs. Simpson. The neighbor gave me your address. I know I could have written or called. But I thought I would just take a chance

41

and see if I could talk to you in person."

Karen paused, looking a little embarrassed. "I'm very sorry to have just barged in like this. And I'm truly sorry for your loss, Mrs. Simpson. I don't know how I could have forgotten to tell you that right away!"

"Merry Christmas, everybody!"

"That's how!" said Mrs. Simpson with a laugh. "I thought I was absentminded before! But George interrupts me so much, I forget what I'm thinking half the time."

"What a bird!" said George.

Everyone laughed, which seemed to please George very much.

But Titus didn't want to let George get them off the subject.

If there's one thing detectives have to be good at, it's listening carefully. And Karen had said a couple of things that Titus wanted to follow up on.

He said to Karen, "Do you mind if I ask you two questions? It might help to clear some things up."

"Sure," said Karen. "Ask away."

"OK," said Titus. "First—who was it who told you to go and see Uncle Henry? And second—what was it that Uncle Henry was keeping for you?"

"Good questions," said Karen. "Unfortunately, the answer to both of them is—I don't know."

11

The Letter

Karen pulled out a letter. "This came for me quite some time ago," she explained. "But I've been gone all summer, so I didn't get it until just now. It says that there's an extremely important packet waiting for me. But it doesn't tell me what it is. It just says that a Mr. Henry Appleby is holding it for me and that if I show him some identification I can claim what is rightfully mine. His instructions are to turn the packet over to me and to explain what it all means. I don't know who the letter is from."

"You mean there's no name on it?" asked Sarah-Jane. "What's the word for that? *Anonymous?* Someone sent you an anonymous letter?"

"No," said Karen. "I didn't say it right. I

didn't mean that there was *no* name on the letter. I meant I didn't *recognize* the name. I don't know who the person is who sent me the letter."

"Why would someone you've never even heard of send you a letter?" asked Timothy. "It doesn't make sense."

"I know," said Karen.

"And what was all that stuff about claiming what is rightfully yours?" asked Titus.

Karen shrugged. "Beats me. But the whole thing got me so curious that I just had to check it out."

The cousins nodded. They understood completely. It was exactly what they would have done. When you're curious about something, what else can you do but check it out?

Karen handed the letter to Mrs. Simpson, who gave a cry of surprise. "Why, I know who this is!" she exclaimed.

"You *do*?" cried Karen and the cousins together.

"Yes," said Mrs. Simpson. "If it's the same Paul Erickson I'm thinking of. He was a good friend of Uncle Henry's. You met him, Titus, remember? We went to visit Uncle Henry, and

Mr. Erickson was there, too. You and he played a game of chess."

"I remember," said Titus. "But isn't he the one who had to go into a nursing home or something?"

"That's right," said Mrs. Simpson. "Except he passed away at the beginning of the summer."

"That must have been just after he gave the packet to Uncle Henry and wrote to Karen," said Titus. "I wonder why he didn't just mail it."

"Maybe he thought this would be safer," said Karen. "Or maybe he wanted Uncle Henry to tell me something in person about it." She turned to Mrs. Simpson. "So you don't know anything about it?"

Mrs. Simpson shook her head sadly. "I *know* I wouldn't have forgotten something like that. But I think Uncle Henry forgot to tell me."

They were all quiet for a moment, thinking about all this. What could be in the mysterious packet? And where was it now?

Their thoughts were interrupted by a loud, sad sigh coming from George. "Fenway all gone," he said. "Fenway all gone."

12

Nonsense

*T*itus couldn't bear to think of George being sad about anything. He went over to the cage and talked softly to him.

George, of course, just loved the attention.

"You're talking nonsense again, you silly old bird," Titus told him affectionately. "The *peanuts* are all gone. Not the *fenway*. Fenway is the name of a person."

George cocked his head and looked at him with interest. It was as if he was politely puzzled over Titus's point of view and wanted to discuss it.

"Hi, Titus."

"Hi, George."

"Hi, George."

Titus laughed and shook his head. How

could a bird who looked so smart get so mixed up about things?

But at the back of Titus's mind, an idea was beginning to take shape. Maybe George *wasn't* talking nonsense. At least not all the time. Maybe at least one of the crazy things he said made perfect sense. Maybe . . .

But the idea wouldn't stay still long enough for Titus to grab it. He knew, though, if he could just be patient it would come to him.

In the meantime, Mrs. Simpson was talking to Karen. "As a matter of fact, we were just on our way over to get started cleaning out my uncle's apartment. Why don't you come with us, Karen? We could look for your mysterious packet. This sounds like a job for the T.C.D.C."

Karen gave a puzzled frown. The cousins knew what was coming. "What's a 'teesy-deesy'?" she asked.

"It's letters," explained Sarah-Jane. "Capital T. Capital C. Capital D. Capital C. It stands for the Three Cousins Detective Club."

Karen's frown turned into a smile. "That's exactly what I need!" she exclaimed.

"Well, now, I've got to warn you," said

Titus. "Don't get your hopes up. We're good but we're not that good."

Timothy and Sarah-Jane looked at him in surprise. What nonsense was this?

But Mrs. Simpson was not the least bit surprised. She knew exactly what Titus meant.

"My uncle was something of a 'clutter bug,'" she explained. "A 'pack rat.' Almost never threw anything away. Looking for Karen's packet will be like looking for a needle in a haystack. I wouldn't be surprised if Uncle Henry hid it in a safe spot and then completely forgot where he put it."

"I wouldn't, either," said Titus. "It's not that Uncle Henry was careless or anything. I mean, if somebody gave him something for safekeeping, Uncle Henry would keep it safe. You can be sure of that. It's just that—Mrs. Simpson is right. He might have forgotten where he put it. And even if he didn't forget, *we* have no idea where to look."

Karen looked disappointed, but she seemed too polite to say so. Titus wanted to make her feel better. "Don't worry," he said. "Even if we don't find your packet today, we'll find it eventually."

Karen nodded, still looking a little disappointed. Titus understood how she felt. If someone had left a packet for him, he would want to find it NOW. TODAY. RIGHT THIS VERY MINUTE. He just wasn't sure they could.

Again, he had the strange feeling that George of all people—uh, birds—held the clue.

But what was it?

13

Needle in a Haystack

"Well, Ti," said Timothy. "You weren't kidding."

The three detective cousins stood together at the door to Uncle Henry's living room, looking around them in despair. It was worse than they thought.

"A needle in a haystack," said Sarah-Jane.

Mrs. Simpson and Karen didn't look any more hopeful than the cousins.

Where, oh where, could the packet be?

At last Mrs. Simpson said, "I guess we should get started. But I don't know *where* to start."

It was at that moment that Titus made everybody jump by pointing across the room and yelling, "Fenways! Of course! Fenways! It makes perfect sense. Why didn't I think of it before? Uncle Henry was a genius. And George! Good old George! What a bird!"

Titus was aware that everyone was looking at him as if he had completely lost his mind.

He knew he'd better try to explain himself.

Titus took a deep breath. "OK. Here's what I think happened. Uncle Henry wanted to help out his friend, but he didn't trust his own memory. However! Parrots have *amazing* memories. They remember people. They remember places. They remember words. I think Uncle Henry deliberately taught the name *Fenway* to George so that every time George came out with it, Uncle Henry would be reminded about Karen's packet."

"That makes sense, Ti," said Timothy. "It really does. But it still doesn't tell us *where* the packet is."

"Yes, it does," said Titus. "Because George doesn't know *Fenway* is the name of a person. He thinks it's the word for peanuts. That's why it made perfect sense when he said, 'Fenway all gone.' "

"Yes!" cried Sarah-Jane. "When George

found the peanuts in your pocket, he kept saying 'Fenway.' "

"My point exactly," said Titus. "And do you remember where I was sitting when that happened?"

Timothy, Sarah-Jane, and Mrs. Simpson thought back.

It was Mrs. Simpson who said, "You were sitting next to the end table that George likes so much. And—Uncle Henry has one just like it."

"Right," said Titus. He pointed across the room. "I think that end table right over there was the spot where George was used to getting his special treat. His cage used to be here, across the room from the table. Just the way it is in your apartment. No wonder he made the connection. He is one smart bird. I think Uncle Henry trained him to associate the word *Fenway* with getting peanuts in his special spot. That way, when George demanded 'fenways,' it would remind Uncle George of where he hid the packet for someone named Fenway."

"The end table!" cried Mrs. Simpson. "My

goodness, Titus! Whatever made you think of that?!"

Titus kind of hated to give the secret away. He knew it would sound so ordinary. He also knew that Timothy and Sarah-Jane would never, ever give up until he told them.

"There are peanut shells on the floor over there," he said.

Without another word, they all rushed across the room and pulled open the drawer of the little end table.

It was empty.

14

The Packet

*T*he drawer wasn't *absolutely* empty, of course. No drawer in Uncle Henry's apartment was. There were a couple of magazines. Some pencils and pens. Notepaper. Rubber bands. Paper clips. A few stamps. A sack of peanuts.

But no packet.

Titus stared at the drawer in disbelief. How could he have been so wrong? It had all made such perfect sense!

"You know," said Sarah-Jane slowly. "A drawer isn't that great of a hiding place. Not *inside* the drawer, anyway." She looked up at Mrs. Simpson. "Do you mind if I dump this stuff out?"

Mrs. Simpson looked around the room

before she answered and laughed. "What can it possibly hurt? Go right ahead."

Sarah-Jane hesitated. "I saw this on a TV show once. Except—I think Ti should be the one to do it."

Titus looked at her and smiled. He had seen the TV show, too. But that wasn't the only reason he was smiling. It was because cousins could be the nicest people in the whole world.

Carefully he dumped out the contents of the drawer and turned it over.

Maybe Uncle Henry had seen the same TV show.

Because taped to the bottom of the drawer was a little packet with the words *For Karen Fenway* written on it.

"EX-cellent!" said Titus.

"Neat-O!" said Timothy.

"So cool!" said Sarah-Jane.

"That is Uncle Henry's handwriting," said Mrs. Simpson, sounding a little choked up.

Carefully Titus removed the packet and handed it to Karen.

Carefully Karen opened it. What they saw inside made them all gasp. It was a gorgeous

piece of jewelry. A pin set with emeralds and
diamonds.

"I don't understand," said Karen. "This
belonged to my grandmother."

15

What a Bird!

*T*he cousins and Mrs. Simpson stared at Karen as if they couldn't believe their ears.

Karen said, "I've never actually seen this brooch. I've seen pictures of it. It disappeared years and years ago, and no one ever knew what happened to it. My father told me my grandmother was devastated. It had belonged to *her* grandmother, I think. Anyway, my grandmother had always said she wanted it to go to her granddaughter. That's me. The only granddaughter in the family. But how in the world did it—?"

"Look!" said Timothy. "There's a letter!"

And so there was. Written in Uncle Henry's handwriting. It said—

Dear Miss Fenway,

I am holding this brooch in safekeeping for you on behalf of my dear friend Paul Erickson. He is not in the best of health and will soon have to enter a nursing home. He wanted to be sure you received this pin, which is rightfully yours. I am writing down what he said so that I can remember to tell it to you. The brooch belonged to your grandmother. But it was stolen many years ago by none other than Mr. Erickson's sister.

He knew nothing of this until recently. He insisted that the brooch be returned to you, but (rightly or wrongly) he didn't trust any of his relatives to do it. So he entrusted it to me. I will keep it in a safe place. And I have a good helper who will never let me forget where I put it.

Very truly yours,
Henry Appleby

"Well!" said Mrs. Simpson, dabbing at her eyes. "My uncle Henry was really something, wasn't he? And that George! What a bird!"

"What a bird!" agreed Titus. "What a bird!"

———

When the cousins got home, Titus's father was just on his way out.

"I am going to the grocery store," he announced grandly. "Is there anything you need? Speak now or forever hold your peace."

Titus raced into the kitchen to check on something.

He opened the cupboard and looked at what he thought of as his "squirrel shelf." Now that he knew George liked them, too, it was more important than ever to keep them in stock.

But it was just as he thought. They were completely out.

"Dad!" he yelled. "Don't forget to pick up a bag of fenways!"

The End

Series for Young Readers*
From Bethany House Publishers

★ ★ ★

THE ADVENTURES OF CALLIE ANN
by Shannon Mason Leppard

Readers will giggle their way through the true-to-life escapades of Callie Ann Davies and her many North Carolina friends.

★ ★ ★

BACKPACK MYSTERIES
by Mary Carpenter Reid

This excitement-filled mystery series follows the mishaps and adventures of Steff and Paulie Larson as they strive to help often-eccentric relatives crack their toughest cases.

★ ★ ★

THE CUL-DE-SAC KIDS
by Beverly Lewis

Each story in this lighthearted series features the hilarious antics and predicaments of nine endearing boys and girls who live on Blossom Hill Lane.

★ ★ ★

RUBY SLIPPERS SCHOOL
by Stacy Towle Morgan

Join the fun as home-schoolers Hope and Annie Brown visit fascinating countries and meet inspiring Christians from around the world!

★ ★ ★

THREE COUSINS DETECTIVE CLUB®
by Elspeth Campbell Murphy

Famous detective cousins Timothy, Titus, and Sarah-Jane learn compelling Scripture-based truths while finding—and solving—intriguing mysteries.

* (ages 7–10)